HAUNTINGS OF
AVALON

HAUNTINGS OF
AVALON

FLO SWANN

HAUNTINGS OF AVALON

iUniverse books may be ordered through booksellers or by contacting:

iUniverse
1663 Liberty Drive
Bloomington, IN 47403
www.iuniverse.com
1-800-Authors (1-800-288-4677)

ISBN: 978-1-5320-7036-5 (sc)
ISBN: 978-1-5320-7035-8 (e)

Library of Congress Control Number: 2019902771

Print information available on the last page.

iUniverse rev. date: 04/03/2019

Introduction

Let me tell you about what keeps me awake at night. Five years ago, I lived through a horrifying experience that started a couple of days after I moved into the Avalon Motel. The only other person who knew about it was my high school sweetheart, Keith Dabney. He was killed three years ago, and since his passing, I struggle every day. This secret I've kept is screaming to come out. There are times when I want to tell someone about the events at the Avalon, but I don't think anyone would believe me.

Writing my story down will help me move on with my life again and set free those trapped souls so they can go to their next lives. It will bring closure to a situation during which I should have made better choices five years ago. I am ready to make it right with the universe.

Moving into the Avalon

I was nineteen years old when I realized that I couldn't live with my mother. On May 12, my mother and I had one of our worst arguments, so that's the day I told my mother I had to move out. I packed a few outfits and some work clothes and called Keith to let him know I was coming over to his parents' house. When I got there, we talked about my situation. Keith let me know about the Avalon Motel out on Highway 31. He said the motel had been turned into sleeping rooms with weekly and monthly rates, so we agreed to ride out to the Avalon and see whether they had rooms for rent. I figured I'd stay there for the summer and give my mother and me a break from each other. I planned on attending college in the fall, and that's when I could move back home.

We drove about three miles out of town and discussed his staying with me if they had a vacancy. We pulled into the parking lot, and I felt relieved Keith had come with me. I started remembering some stories I had heard about the place.

I knocked on the office door, and an older man answered. He looked me up and down before asking me whether he could help me. I motioned for Keith to get out of the car. We stepped into the office while the man went behind the counter.

"What can I do for you today?" he asked.

"I need a place to stay for the summer," I replied.

"Okay, I have a room vacant. Fill this card out, and I will show you the room," he said.

I filled out the card, and then Keith and I followed the manager to room 1.

We stepped into what looked like a retro '50s kind of motel room. The manager said, "I have replaced the old box spring and mattress. You'll be the first one to sleep on it."

I looked around the room and said, "Okay, I can do this."

The manager walked toward the doorway, saying, "Let's go get you some keys." We followed him back to the office.

The manager excused himself as he entered the back room to retrieve the keys. Keith and I smiled at each other, as we always had a knack for knowing what the other was thinking. I could tell by the look in his eyes that this was going to be a hot, steamy night.

"Let me introduce myself. My name is Jerry Lewis," he said as he handed me the two keys. "Now, Rita, we will not tolerate loud parties on the property. If you get too loud and I get a complaint, you will be evicted. The rent is a hundred twenty-five dollars a week, due on Fridays. Do you have any questions?"

"Is it okay to have a minifridge and microwave in there?" I asked.

"Yeah, that's okay. We have a deposit of thirty dollars that's nonrefundable and due right now. I need a hundred fifty-five, and you can move in." Keith helped me out and paid the first week's rent.

As we got in the car to drive away, I called my mom to let her know I had found a place to stay for the summer. We both had cooled down, and she seemed okay. She made me promise I would come over for breakfast in the morning so we could talk. Now that I look back on it, my mother was trying to get me to make better choices.

Keith helped me move in, letting me use his minifridge and microwave for the room. We had a memorable first night at the Avalon. We smoked some tree, and he played a song he'd written on his acoustic guitar. Keith was my first love. We got together when we were freshmen. He helped me through so much shit and listened to me when my mother pissed me off. He was my everything through all my growing pains. I'm a better person today because of him, except for this secret I've kept all these years.

June 1 was the kickoff for the battle of the bands in our tristate area. Keith and his bandmates started preparing for the event back at Christmas. They finally came up with Skitch as the name of the band. The big event was two weeks away, and Keith was working full-time at Mom's Music, which meant I was alone most of the time. That was okay with me, as I always encouraged Keith to pursue his musical dreams. You know, who didn't want a rock star boyfriend?

The Avalon was only three miles down Highway 31 from the Seventy-Six Truck Stop where I had just started working. Tara, my best friend, helped me get the job. Her uncle was the day-shift cook and the best short-order cook I ever worked with. He kept it rolling, and we made great tips. I would work six or seven hours on any day of the week and leave with $100 to $125 in my pocket. Of course, my mom always told me to save for my future. I listened and started a cash jar that I put $40 a day in. I saved more than $1,000 in the weeks I lived in room 1.

Tara kept me busy after work, as we would hang out at her house a lot. Sandy, Tara's mom, was a great person. She was easy to talk to and fun to hang out with. Sandy was hippy-like. She believed in peace for humanity. She taught me about karma and how it works in the universe and gave me a good understanding of the laws of attraction. Sandy was the first person to expose me to those teachings, and I live by them today. It's one of the reasons this secret I've packed around the past five years is killing me.

I started having dreams that I couldn't remember many details about. I would see a young blonde woman getting ready for a date. It seemed as though she was trying to decide which dress to wear, maybe. Even though I couldn't remember the dreams, I'd wake up feeling drained, almost like I hadn't slept at all.

Tara told me one morning that I had huge bags under my eyes. I barely made it to work on time because I'd been in a deep sleep before the alarm went off. That was the first dream I remember any detail from. The blonde had on a purple dress with her hair in a bouffant style. I watched her apply her makeup, and she looked so excited. She studied herself in an old waterfall vanity mirror before leaving her bedroom. She waited on a porch swing as her date drove up in an El Camino. He got out of the car and opened the passenger door for her. I could see his stature—very tall with broad shoulders. He had dark hair and was well dressed in a nice suit and shiny shoes, but it was too dark for me to see his face. Then I woke up. I scrambled to get myself to work with a minute to spare. I felt sluggish all morning, and Tara was right about the bags under my eyes; I'd never had sacks like that before. Stacy, our manager, gave me some Preparation H for the bags, and it worked great. Thirty minutes after I applied a small amount under my eyes, my bags were gone.

After work, Tara and I came back to Avalon, and I told her about the dream. Tara suggested a few ideas about where this girl in the dream came from. "Maybe she's a customer at the diner, or maybe you saw her in a commercial on TV." We smoked on my pipe and laughed about it.

The battle of the bands started on a Friday night. Skitch was lined up to be the last performance of the night, which made Keith nervous.

Every band was killer and showcased tremendous talent. I pep talked him before they took to the stage, and they won the first round of the battle! We were all so pumped to come back for the next battle. We partied like rock stars that night.

I went to work Saturday morning with no sleep, but I made it through my shift. I went to my room directly after work to catch a few hours of sleep. Keith was there waiting for me. I fell asleep right away in his arms. It was the most peaceful sleep I'd had in days. How I needed that.

Saturday night was terrific. Skitch took the stage around ten o'clock and won the 2012 battle of the bands! This was the opportunity of a lifetime for Skitch. A record company executive walked up to the band afterward and handed each member one of his cards. The looks on all their faces, filled with exuberant enthusiasm, was an extreme joy to witness. I still have such pride in what they accomplished in three years, before the bus crash.

By the following Monday, offers for gigs started pouring in. They reached a level of local fame. A news crew did a piece on the band later that week.

Haunting Dreams

Three weeks into crashing at the Avalon, I was feeling more at home. Keith and I made a pact to spend one night a week together, no matter what. I asked my mom if I could use the extra DVD player and the Xbox 360, and I packed up my big hookah. I made room 1 a cool crib to chill with my buddies.

My friend Lizzy reached out to me because she was having boyfriend issues. She needed a place to get away for a couple of days. I hadn't laid eyes on her since graduation night. I was happy to see her and catch up.

All through high school Lizzy and I had the same classes. We spent many hours cramming for tests in my bedroom at home. We weren't the best students, as we could have applied ourselves more. But we maintained a C average. Yes, we did smoke a lot of trees. Oh, the good ol' days.

Lizzy came out to the Avalon driving a Beetle Bug convertible. It was a sweet little car and a five-speed too. When she got out of the car, I almost didn't recognize her. She'd been chunky all through school, but Lizzy had lost at least fifty pounds in one year. She still had her spark of sarcasm that I remembered all too well.

We caught up about the past year until midnight. I had to be at work by six thirty in the morning. We lay down on the bed. She fell asleep instantly, while I lay there for an hour before I found my slumber.

I dreamed of the blonde and the tall man again. It was very vivid, almost like being right there with them. He picked her up in his El Camino. She was wearing a pink dress with her hair down. I witnessed their whole date. She was enjoying his company, smiling and giggling. I still could not see his face. His body gestures indicated he was smitten by her. They left a restaurant on foot and walked to a park in the town square. They strolled around the park, and then he took her home. He walked her to the porch, and they kissed good night.

My alarm clock woke me. I got right up so I wouldn't hit the snooze button. The dream was fresh in my mind on the way to work. I started my day with an energy drink to keep up with an early breakfast rush. I left work $159 richer. We'd worked our asses off for it.

Lizzy stayed with me for the next three nights, and I had the same dream each night, except the dresses the girl wore were different colors. I told Lizzy all about these stupid dreams. She said it meant something. Maybe a spirit was communicating with me. I agreed to that possibility because before moving to the Avalon, I didn't recall dreaming at all.

I talked to Tara that morning, and she said I needed to see a psychic. She knew of one across the river. Tara made a call to see whether the psychic had an opening. After work, we picked up Lizzy and drove to the psychic's house. She lived in a beautiful part of town, in a big three-story house.

I felt unsure as we walked into her house. Tara did all the explaining about what I was experiencing. She led us to a parlor and motioned for us to sit at a table.

"My name is Isabella. Please relax. Tension distracts me," she said. "It is all about the vibes I receive from you." She went on to ask a few questions while she held my hand. I answered honestly, trying not to give too much detail. I was a skeptic.

Isabella seemed to be meditating for a minute or two, and then she said, "I'm not clear on the reasons this young woman is showing you these visions. I would have to come to the location to be clear. I am certain of one thing. She wants to show you why. To have skepticism is delaying her message."

I asked Isabella when she could travel to the Avalon, and she said it would be next week. She handed me her card and told me to call her on Tuesday. I paid her the twenty-dollar fee, and we thanked her for her time.

We all agreed that was a waste of time. You never know until you try, is what I believe. On the way back home, we decided to stop at the Seafood Place for dinner. We discussed my sleep issues, and Tara suggested a mild sleeping pill. I said okay to that idea. Maybe I could get some real sleep without getting trashed on booze and tree.

The last night Lizzy stayed with me, she told me why she had lost so much weight in a year. She had been hooked on heroin and done rehab. She'd been clean for two months now. The boyfriend was the dealer she stopped buying from. He'd been stalking her and wanted his money for the last batch she got from him before rehab. I asked how much she owed, and she replied that it was $500. I made an instant decision to give her the money. We took a ride to my bank's ATM, and I pulled the cash out of my savings account. I told her to pay me back when she could. I couldn't live with myself if this man hurt her over it when I could help her. When she left me that day, I never thought she would turn up dead in a cornfield a week later. I wish I could have saved her somehow.

Keith stayed with me for two days after the news of Lizzy's death. I called off work those days. I was so heartsick over Lizzy that I honestly could not function. Keith took good care of me, yet he gave me room to express my grief. I was emotionally and physically exhausted. I took two Ambien the second night Keith stayed with me. I slept for fourteen hours before waking up to empty my bladder. Keith went down to Seventy-Six for a large cup of coffee and some doughnuts for us. I was lying on the bed when he came back, feeling hungover from the Ambien. He fixed my coffee with lots of sugar and told me to sit at the table with him. We ate our doughnuts in silence before I thanked him for being there for me. He replied with "No thanks needed." He said it was his job to be there for me. He told me he would always be with me, even in our next lives. I wish he didn't have to leave me in this one.

I went back to work feeling well rested. That was a good thing because we had two busloads of customers come in for lunch. They were all senior citizens, who are known to not tip well. We worked hard to serve them all.

Tara and I had just finished all the chores for our shift when our relief came in. We decided we deserved a treat for our hard work. Tara wanted us to get our nails and toes done at the mall. I suggested we take Sandy and I would treat her for just being the awesome person she was.

Later on, I went home to see my mom. She kept insisting I move back home. Classes started in three weeks, and she wanted time with me. We talked about the reasons I moved out, and for once, she admitted that she nagged way too much. I had kept up my end of the deal we made after graduation. She agreed to let me have a year of freedom. I would work, party, and rest my brain from learning. But she regularly lectured and nagged me about my future. Hey, here's a news flash—you've got to give a person a chance to fuck up first before you can start the nagging. I left my mom feeling all right about our talk, and that I would be ready to come home when it was time.

I walked down to the office at Avalon to pay my rent. Jerry Lewis was sitting outside, drinking a beer. I decided to ask some questions about my room. He looked leisurely, so I sat down on the curb for a chat. "How are you today?" I asked.

He smiled and said, "Real good. It's Friday. My work is done for the week as long as everybody pays their rent."

I chuckled. "Can I ask you a question?" I turned around so I could see his facial expressions.

He nodded. "What's on your mind, young lady?"

"Well, I was wondering who lived in my room before me."

He took a big swig of his beer. "An old guy named Harold. Why you ask?"

I said casually, "I was just wondering. How old is this place?"

He said, "Rooms one through eleven, along with the office, were built in 1951 and the second half in 1960. You know Avalon was here long before I-65 was built. Highway 31 was the main road north to south before I-65 came along. You grow up here?" he asked.

"Yes, graduated from Silver Creek in 2011."

He finished his beer and was reaching in his cooler for another. "You want one?" he asked.

"Sure I'll have one. How long you been here?"

He smiled and said, "I took over back in ninety-five. This place was a mess back then. Lots of stories about what went down here back then."

"Yeah," I replied.

I drank my beer, and he said, "You old enough to drink beer, girl?" while he offered another, and I took it.

"Thank you. Nope, I'm nineteen, but I won't tell anybody you gave me a beer." I smiled big at him with a wink.

"You're my kind of girl. Yeah, Harold lived here forty-three years in that same room. He was a nice old guy. He passed away back in January. He was a highly decorated Vietnam vet. I used to shoot the shit with him on Fridays, have a few beers, and talk about what's wrong with kids today. I miss him. God rest his soul. He came back from the war. Since he had no family around here, he landed at the Avalon and stayed."

I know I looked surprised. "He really lived here forty-three years?" I asked in disbelief. Who lives in a motel room that long? All I could say was, "Wow!"

Jerry Lewis stood up to stretch. "Do you want a shot of Wild Turkey? I will bring it out here for us." He walked into his office and then came out with two shot glasses and a pint of Turkey.

"Yeah, I can drink one with ya," I said as he poured the shots.

He lit a cigarette and sat back down in his chair. "In ninety-five this place was a mess. We had prostitutes, drug dealers, and lot lizards running around. The worst of society were up in here. It took me a few weeks to get rid of them all and clean up from the scum they left behind. But Harold stayed on. He retired from his job after thirty years and lived peacefully until I found him that Friday."

I perked up. "Did he die in that room?"

Jerry Lewis cracked up laughing at my question. "No, he wasn't dead—but almost. He had a stroke and was in bad shape. I got him help, and he made it to the next day, then passed in the hospital," he replied.

Jesus, I'm glad he didn't die there, I thought. I had a second shot and started feeling Turkey creeping up on me. I stood up. "Thank you for the buzz and the talk. I'm ready for a nap," I said.

"You are welcome any time to come down and sit awhile," Jerry replied.

I walked down to my room and loaded up my hookah. The third big hit, and I was toasted. I lay back on the bed and fell asleep.

I wanted to wake up, but I couldn't. I could see that same El Camino pulling into the driveway. I looked around, not sure where I was. The tall man got out of the El Camino, and then stepping around to the passenger side, he opened the door. The blonde woman stepped out. This time she had a long white dress on. The vision was so vivid. It was a wedding dress. The man picked her up, carried her through a doorway, and shut the door with his foot. As I looked around, I realized where we were. Room 1—oh shit …

My alarm went off for ten minutes before I heard it. My head was pounding. *Oh, why did I drink that Wild Turkey?* I took a quick shower, got dressed, and jumped into my Mustang. Then I headed to work. That dream was all that was on my mind. Tara asked me if I was all right a few times that morning. I was off my game, hungover, and hungry. I had to eat on the run since we had a busy breakfast.

The business died in the afternoon, so I asked Tara if I could go home. I felt bad to bail on her, but I was not worth a dime. Tara said, "Don't worry about it. Go rest."

She promised to stop by the Avalon later to check on me. I apologized before I left work. "I'm a sack of shit today."

Keith had to cancel our night together that week. His grandma was in the hospital, so his mom needed his help. I was disappointed, but I assured him that I understood. I told him I loved him and I would call him after work the next day.

My phone needed charging, so I walked over to the dresser to put it on the charger. Something caught my attention in the mirror. I looked at the mirror, and I saw an image of green eyes. I took a second look. A woman's face was staring back at me. Her eyes were as green as mine, blonde hair … I shook my head and looked at the mirror again. The image was gone. My knees buckled. I almost fell. I thought, *I have smoked too much tree lately.*

Tara stopped by after work as she promised. I didn't let her stay long because I needed sleep. I told her I was all right and I would see her in the morning. I walked out to her car and took the aspirin she bought me. I thanked her and promised to sleep well and be on top of my game in the morning.

I showered and fixed a sandwich for dinner. I avoided looking in the mirror. The green eyes were creepy as hell. I couldn't shake this feeling in my stomach. I talked myself down. I didn't want to vomit. I got in bed and closed my eyes tight, and I drifted off to sleep.

I heard screaming, a woman begging for him to stop. I opened the door. The tall man was raping the blonde woman. He was behind her, pulling her hair, pounding into her as she cried. He put his big hands around her neck. He was choking her. She stopped crying as he seemed to climax inside her. He let her go, and she flopped facedown on the bed. He sat there and looked stunned. Then he tried to shake her, asking her to wake up. He started moaning as he realized she was hurt badly. I just stood there, watching him. He walked over to a chair and picked up her white dress. He was sobbing so loud I covered my ears. He had just murdered his new bride, a pretty young blonde. I was frozen, I wanted to run out the door, but my legs wouldn't move. He picked up her body, holding her tight. I don't think he meant to hurt her.

I opened my eyes to Keith shaking me. I sat up and grabbed him. I had never felt so terrified. He wrapped his arms around me. "It's okay, baby. I'm here," he said in a soothing voice. He held me until I was ready to talk.

Love and Loss

The next day after work, I went to my room, hoping to find Keith waiting there. He left me a note on the dresser stating that his grandma had passed away. All this death around me was devastating. I was starting to feel numb, unable to cope with it all.

I cleaned up and went to see my mom. I honestly felt that I needed my mommy. I can't explain it, but I don't recall the last time I needed her like that.

I hung out with my mom, talking for a couple of hours. I asked her if she wanted to go to Lizzy's funeral with me. "Of course," she said, "Lizzy was like a second daughter to me."

We reminisced about Lizzy and her best sarcastic phrases. We laughed hard, and I started to feel better. "Laughter is good for the soul," is what my daddy used to say before he had the fatal heart attack right there on the basement steps, back in 2010.

I went up to my room. I wanted to gather all my pictures of Lizzy. I sat at my vanity and was startled by my reflection. I had slight bags, with dark circles under my eyes. I looked older than my mom! That had me tripping for a second.

I rummaged through my closet for a dress to wear to Lizzy's service and Keith's grandma's too. I packed my stuff up and then walked down the hallway to my mom's room. A memory flooded my mind of Daddy chasing Mom around the upstairs. I could hear her laughter. I will never forget the chill that ran up my spine while I stood there in the hallway.

As I drove back to the Avalon that evening, I decided to move back home next Friday. With two weeks before my classes started, it would be enough time to get myself together.

I arrived back at the Avalon to find Keith waiting for me. He hugged me tightly, with tears in his eyes. His grandma had had severe arthritis, so she no longer could walk or feed herself. I know that tore him up inside every time he visited her at the rehab facility. We talked about it a few times, and he knew the end was coming. My heart ached for him. We lay on the bed awhile and held each other.

Monday was Keith's grandma Dabney's service. There were so many people in attendance. She was highly thought of by those who knew her. Keith learned so much about her younger years. Her parents sent her to Europe for the summers to stay with one of her aunts. She was fluent in French and a talented artist. We learned that all the paintings in her house were her own work. Arthritis had stopped her from painting years ago. Keith didn't even know what her name was besides Grandma. He said he would never have guessed it was Imma Jean. She was such a worldly lady, with an old country name.

Lizzy's body was held for over two weeks before they would release it for burial. Her autopsy revealed she was stabbed seventeen times in the face and chest. Evidence showed she was killed, and then the body was moved to the cornfield. Lizzy had no traces of heroin or meth in her system. I felt proud of her for staying clean at least. All those stab wounds suggested it was a crime of intense anger. What the hell could a nineteen-year-old girl do to somebody to be butchered liked that? Of course, she had a closed casket for the service that Wednesday.

Our entire class came to pay their respects to Lizzy. She had been bright and funny, and we had lots of stories to share about our friend. Lizzy had been friendly to anyone and helpful when we needed her. Most people that day agreed Lizzy was the last person they would've thought to become an addict and die a brutal death like that.

Tara didn't do well with the funeral. She couldn't control her emotions. That was Tara's first experience of losing someone close to her. Before that day, I didn't know she had never been to a funeral. I felt so sorry for Tara. I was so caught up in my own grief that I wasn't there for her till the day of the funeral. My mom was Tara's rock for the day, one of the many times I admired my mom's strength.

The Tunnel

Jerry Lewis was sitting outside with his cooler of beer. I walked down to visit and let him know I would be leaving Friday. He asked why, and I told him about my agreement with my mom to go to school. He was curious if I had been happy staying there, and I assured him I liked my stay for the summer. I did spread my wings while I was away from my mom.

I didn't say anything about the dreams to him. I don't think he would have believed me if I did. Besides, I thought the blonde would rest well now since she showed me what happened to her. Or at least she could move on to the light and set her soul free to its next life.

I went to my room and started gathering my stuff. I had to work the next morning, and Skitch had a gig at the Bar for the next three nights. I packed most of my things in my Mustang's trunk. Friday I would go to work and turn my key in. I was looking forward to my bedroom at home, where I belonged.

I wore myself out getting all my stuff packed in my trunk. I showered, then settled down in bed. I called Keith to check on him and his mom. He said they were okay. His mom took a nerve pill before going to bed. She would be knocked out all night. She needed the rest, and so did I. I went to sleep the instant my head hit the pillow. My bladder woke me at a quarter after two in the morning. As I sat on the toilet, I felt a cold draft across my feet on the floor. The sensation gave me chills all over, just like in the hallway at home. I wiped and flushed and hurried back to bed. I wrapped up in my blanket and collected my three hours of sleep before the alarm.

The blonde girl appeared in front of me and motioned for me to follow her. I didn't have a clue where I was. Was that a dim light on down the hallway? Looking at the walls, I touched them to find out they were made of dirt. I was underground! She turned to me and said, "Come on." She had her wedding dress on. It was torn and tattered. We approached a light coming from the end of the tunnel. It felt like we were in a cave. I saw stalactites hanging from the ceiling. The light was coming from a fire in the middle of the cavern. I looked at her as I walked toward the fire. She was pointing to the floor. I thought, *Oh fuck, are those bones?* There were piles of them against the wall around the firepit. *Oh shit.* I started to run back down the tunnel, tripping over something.

"Rita!" the blonde screamed. As I sat up in bed, my hands were trembling. I was profusely sweating over my whole body. At a quarter after five, the alarm sounded, and I was wide awake. I sat there a minute. I was tangled up in the blanket. I was thankful to be awake. What a fucked-up dream. I had to shower the sweat off my body and then put myself together. I hoped Tara was okay today. She couldn't stop the tears yesterday.

I pulled in to Seventy-Six's parking lot, and Tara was there already. I felt relieved as I walked in. We had our usual breakfast together, coffee and doughnuts, before we took over the floor. I studied Tara's face. Her eyes were swollen.

"Are you feeling better?" I asked her.

She gave me a half smile. "Yeah, I'm sorry I cried so much."

"Oh baby, you're okay," I said, hugging her. "My dad's funeral was my first one. I remember feeling the sadness in everyone's heart in the room, and it was too heavy to bear. That feeling stayed with me a long time."

Tara said, "Lizzy will always be here in my heart. I hope they fry the ones who took her life away!"

"Me too." I agreed. We had a busy morning. We made over a hundred dollars each in tips. We had the diner clean and stocked for the next shift before one o'clock in the afternoon.

To kill time, I chatted with Gus at the counter. Gus had been a breakfast regular for the past thirty years. He had told me so much about the local history. He remembered dirt roads in his childhood. Today he was talking about Al Capone coming down from Chicago to gamble and visit cathouses by the river. Listening to Gus's stories made me think about what subject to major in, and at that moment, I decided journalism would be my future occupation.

Tara agreed to hang out at the Avalon after work. I had some chronic tree, and we deserved an excellent high today. I wanted to make sure I got all my stuff too. We entered the room, which felt like it was a hundred degrees. I turned on the full air blast. We smoked my tree, and I told Tara about the dream I had that morning. We were both trippin'. A ghost showed me in my dreams what happened to her. I wanted Tara to come with us for Skitch's gig at the Bar tonight, but she just wanted to go home. I walked her out to her car, telling her I would be back home tomorrow. I did miss my bed …

Keith came out to the Avalon to pick me up for the gig. I wore my free-flowing white sundress with beige wedges. I curled my hair and applied some makeup. Keith's eyes lit up when I opened the door. He loved to see me dolled up. He had his Levi's on with a Saliva concert tee. I loved my rock-star boyfriend.

I walked to the bathroom to make sure I had all my belongings and took a last check in the mirror. As I was coming out of the doorway, I tripped over something on the floor and fell facedown. Keith jumped up, asking if I was all right. My ankle was twisted a bit. As he helped me to my feet, we looked to see what I tripped over. We moved an old area rug to see the flooring underneath. I turned on the overhead light to see a cellar door in the floor. Keith pulled it up, and there were steps. We debated where the steps led to. We had a couple of hours before we had to leave for the gig. Keith took my hand and stepped down first. I grabbed my phone to use as a flashlight and followed Keith.

At the end of the staircase, it was pitch black. I turned the light on to see we were standing in a small cellar. That was when I noticed the tunnel.

I started trembling and said, "Oh my God, Keith I dreamed about a tunnel last night!"

I took the lead as we walked on down the tunnel. I will never forget that feeling in my stomach as we approached the end of the tunnel. I stopped at the entrance of a cavern. "Keith, in my dream there were piles of bones stacked up around a big fire it."

He pulled my hand up, so that my light shined on my face, and said, "Are you serious?"

"The blonde was raped and murdered right here at the Avalon. She showed me what happened to her in my dreams."

We were both shaking as he grabbed my hand to comfort me. We looked around with the small beam of light from my phone. Stalactites were hanging from the ceiling, and I brought the light to the ground. Rocks made a circle on the floor, and a skull was lying next to a rock. I dropped my phone and screamed. I pulled Keith's shirt and started to run. He picked up my phone and shined it down on the floor.

"Rita, stop!" he yelled, shining the light on my face.

"I want to get out of here." I started crying.

"Okay," he said. We made our way back up the steps to the room. We placed the rug over the cellar door and left the Avalon. We made a pact never to tell anyone else what we found in that cave.

Keith and I talked about that summer a few times, and he believed keeping that secret was for the best. The battle of the bands was the start of Skitch's fame. They landed a record deal the fall of 2012. While I went upstate to college, the band started touring the United States.

In the spring of 2015, which was my junior year, my world stopped. Keith and Hayden were killed when a semi hit the bus as it jackknifed down a mountain in Tennessee. They were on the way home for a few days. Keith had given me a beautiful engagement ring for Christmas 2014, and we had plans for the wedding in the summer of 2016. I have struggled with getting past my grief ever since that fateful St. Patrick's Day, when my everything was taken.

I dropped out of school and moved back home after Keith's funeral. I sat in my bedroom for five months playing video games before I could pull myself together and rejoin society. My mom was my rock. She waited for me to join life again with love and patience. Shortly after, I got a job in a factory in town.

I hung out with Tara from time to time but mostly stayed in my room. I felt cheated of the life I should have had. I felt regretful for the secret I'd been keeping. All those bones in that cave were people taken away from their families. It wasn't right to keep the secret, and in doing so, I suffered terrible karma. I knew it was time to make it right. I know now that's why the spirit of a young, pretty blonde revealed her story to me—to set her soul free from the Avalon Motel. The next day I planned to research and figure out the blonde's name from my dreams. It was time to tell the world about that tunnel and where it led to.

Moving Forward

"Good morning, Mama," I said as I walked into the kitchen.

She was sitting at the island reading *Time* magazine. "Good morning. Would you like some coffee?" she asked, looking up at me. "You look alive today. I like that, baby. You feeling better?"

"Yeah, I do. I've done some soul searching, and I'm ready to unburden all that weighs heavy on me. I know Keith wouldn't want me to waste away in my bedroom." I poured a big cup of coffee and sat down across from her. "I took a two-week leave of absence from work starting Monday," I announced to her.

"Okay. May I ask why? Please tell me you're going back to school," Mom said.

"Well, yes, I do want to finish my degree. I need some time for myself first," I replied.

I could tell by the look on her face that she was processing and searching for words that I wouldn't perceive as nagging. "Mom, I promise I will finish my last three semesters. I don't want to go upstate to finish. I can do it here at the local university, or maybe online. I will check with an adviser on campus," I said.

She agreed for me to stay home for school. I walked around to her stool and bear-hugged her. "Thank you. I couldn't ask for a better mother than you. Your love and patience have gotten me through the past three years. I'm ready to pick my life up and start participating again."

Mom told me to take my time, with the exception that I had to be enrolled for classes by the spring semester. I agreed to take care of it.

First thing on my agenda was to ride out to the Seventy-Six truck stop to talk with Tara. She had received her promotion to general manager a year earlier. She oversaw all operations. I was thinking about coming back to work in the diner and quitting my current nowhere, shit job. I also hoped to see Gus there having breakfast.

I entered the building through the diner's entrance, and sure enough, there Gus was, sitting on his usual stool at the counter. I sat down on the empty seat beside him, and after a moment, he recognized me.

"Hello, young lady," he said with a big smile.

"Hello, young man," I replied.

Gus turned his stool to face me and asked, "How are you? I've wondered about you many times." He had a concerned look in his eyes.

I smiled and said, "I am getting better each day. I'm ready to finish school and make a life for myself."

I ordered some eggs and bacon and continued to chat with Gus. I asked him if he knew of caves or caverns around Highway 31. He said no and then told me to try the register office in the county courthouse. They might have what I was looking for.

Gus and I finished our breakfast, and I attempted to pay for his. Then he caught me. He insisted that he would pay for our meals. "A real man would never let a woman pay for his meal. Don't ever give your time to a cheap-ass man. You are much too pretty of a woman to accept that from any man. You hear me?" he said in a serious tone.

"Yes, sir," I answered.

Gus patted my back as he got up from the stool. "Come to see me again, Rita."

I nodded. "Yes, sir, I will."

I observed how busy the diner was, and for a Friday at eight thirty, it was slow. There used to be a group of older men here every weekday morning for breakfast and social time.

"Hi there, Rita. How are you today?" Tara said as she walked up to the counter.

"I'm good. I had a delicious breakfast with Gus, and I came to ask you if you're free to hang out after work today."

"Yes, I can. I should be done here by 3:00 p.m. or so," Tara replied.

"Cool. Text me after you get home, and I will come over," I said as I hopped down from the bar stool.

"Why are you here instead of at work, may I ask?" She chuckled.

"I took a leave of absence for two weeks. I'm also going back to school in the spring semester, but I'm going to attend the university here in town. I will tell you all about it when I see you later." I gave her a quick hug.

"Okay, see ya later," she said.

I stopped at the Avalon on the way back to town. I pulled in front of the office and parked. As I got out of the Mustang, Jerry Lewis came strolling up the sidewalk. "Hello, young lady. What brings you by? I hope you have time for a sit-down." Jerry asked as I walked toward him.

"Yes, I came by to visit with you," I replied.

Jerry brought two chairs out to the sidewalk for us to sit, and his cooler. "Would you like a beer? I have Cokes also if you would like one," he offered.

"I will have a Coke, please. It's a bit early for beer." I laughed as I sat down in a fold-up chair.

"Let me get ya the Coke. You want a cup of ice? They are cold though," he said.

"I'll just drink out of the can, sir." I got a cigarette out of my bag and lit it up while I waited for my cold drink.

Jerry asked me what I'd been up to since Keith's funeral. "Working an assembly line for the past two and a half years," I said, answering his question with a smile.

He studied my face for a moment and then said, "You look well."

"Thank you, Jerry Lewis. I am ready to pick up my life and start living again. I'm going to finish my degree in journalism. I want to start back in January," I said.

"Glad to hear that you're moving forward. I know losing the love of your life was devastating. He would want you to keep on truckin'," Jerry said, drinking his beer.

"I was wondering if you have anyone staying in room one," I said.

"Yeah, they said they were leaving next week. Why do you ask?" he said.

"Next weekend we have some guests in from upstate, and I want to crash somewhere else for that couple of days," I answered.

"Okay, hon, if it's open, you can rent it for the weekend."

"Thank you. I will be here next Friday," I assured him. "I really need to fly on down the road. I promised my mom I would take care of some chores at the house. Thanks for the Coke," I said. Jerry stood up and hugged me. "You're welcome, young lady. I will see ya soon." He walked to my car and opened the door for me. "You drive safe now."

"I will see ya, Jerry."

I arrived back at the house in time for lunch. Mom's Jeep was gone, so I went in and made a tuna sandwich. I sat at the kitchen island to eat when Sheena came running down the stairs to see who was home. She greeted me with lots of licks and then wanted a bite of my sandwich, I could see it in her puppy dog eyes.

Sheena was a Great Dane we had gotten a few weeks earlier. She was now seventeen weeks old. She was the most beautiful puppy, and she looked identical to Scooby-Doo. She helped me snap out of the depression state I'd been in the past three years.

I decided to take charge of my future since I was left behind in this life. What else was there to do but live it to the fullest? I was ready for that now. At twenty-four years of age, I had so much more to do. Keith and I had had plans to take lots of vacations to different places. A career in journalism would take me to those places. Keith would always be with me everywhere I went.

Tara texted me after she left the Seventy-Six for the day. I headed over to her house on foot for the exercise. It was only four blocks down the street. Autumn was starting to settle in, and trees were at the peak of their vibrant colors.

I approached their house and saw the old scarecrow on the front porch. It took me back to the first Halloween Tara, Lizzy, and I got to trick-or-treat without our parents. Good times …

I knocked on the back door. Sandy let me in. "Rita, how are you, honey?" She hugged me.

"I'm getting better," I replied. I followed Sandy to the living room, where Tara was sitting on the couch.

"Hey," she said with a smile.

"Hey, I see y'all redecorated. I like it," I said, looking around the room. "When did y'all do all the updates?" I asked.

"It been a year ago now," Sandy answered with a chuckle.

"It's been that long since I came over here?" I asked. "I'm sorry …"

"Honey, it's okay. No apology needed. We understand," Sandy assured me.

"Have a seat, Rita. Would you like some wine?" Tara asked as she went to the kitchen.

"Yes, please," I said. My stomach felt all knotted up. I sat down, and Tara handed me a glass of red wine. I took a big drink.

After the second glass of wine, I felt ready to tell Tara what was on my mind. "Remember when I spent the summer staying at the Avalon?"

"Yes," she answered.

I took a deep breath and asked, "Remember those dreams I had about the blonde girl?" Tara nodded, wondering where this was going. "The last night I slept there, I dreamed of a tunnel under the room. In the dream, the blonde showed me where her body was. In a cavern, she showed me piles of bones around a firepit," I said.

"Yeah, I remember you telling me about all those dreams," she said.

"Well, after you left the Avalon, Keith came to pick me up for that gig Skitch had that weekend. I wore a dress with wedge heels, and I tripped over something on the floor and fell facedown. Keith and I pulled an old rug up to see what I tripped over. There was an old cellar door with warped boards. Keith opened it up, and we found steps going down under the room. It was pitch black, so we used our phones for flashlights. We went down and found a tunnel leading to a cavern. We found a big firepit with piles of bones circling around it."

Tara and Sandy had looks of disbelief on their faces. I would too if I heard this story. "Honey, are you sure of what you saw?" Sandy asked.

"Oh yeah, I'm pretty sure of what Keith and I found down there," I said. "You two are the first ones I have told about this. Keith and I agreed never to tell anyone else." They were silent, trying to grasp the whole story. "I can't go on until I expose what happened to the blonde. We should have never stayed quiet about it all. I have to let go of all this and give closure to that girl's family," I said. "I feel relief since I decided to do the right thing. I am ready to make this right so that I can go on with my life." Tears came that I couldn't hold back.

They both embraced me while I cried it out. I had not let it all out for quite some time, and I had a lot built up inside. During the past seven years I had lost three people who meant the world to me.

"You know, Rita, we both have missed having you active in our lives. We have waited for you to find your way through your grief," Sandy said, while handing me a box of tissues.

I blew my nose so I could breathe again. "I'm grateful to have you guys and my mom. Thank you for being my friend, even when I was shut down from the world," I said looking at Tara. "I know I haven't been any fun the past three years. I'm ready to move forward now and be there for everyone again. You know, participate in all my relationships again," I said.

"We welcome you back," Sandy replied.

"I feel so much lighter now. I'm going to make it right for the blonde, may she rest in peace. Then I'm going back to school and finish my degree in journalism," I declared.

"Congrats on pulling your head out of the sand. I need my childhood bestie back full-time in my life," Tara said.

I drank too much wine the previous night, and I was feeling it that morning. Tara drove me home because I couldn't walk a straight line if my life depended on it. That was the first drink I'd had in three years. Even though my head hurt a bit, I felt good emotionally, and my mind was clear—ready to make a plan.

As I showered, my mind went into overdrive about how to find out who the blonde girl and her killer were. Maybe Jerry Lewis could answer some of my questions. First, I thought I would try to catch Gus having his breakfast at Seventy-Six's diner.

"Rita, are you awake?" Mom yelled up the stairs.

"Yeah, I'll be down in a minute," I answered. I sat down at my vanity to apply a bit of eye makeup. Looking good is part of feeling good, and I loved the jumpsuit I had on. It still fit my curves perfectly, like Keith said the day he bought it for me.

Mom made pancakes for us. They were delicious with the strawberry topping. "You are beautifully put together today. What's on your agenda?" she asked.

"Get signed up for classes in January. Then go shopping for new clothes with Tara later," I said in between bites.

"Okay, sounds good. I have something for you." She handed me a pink envelope from her purse. I opened it and pulled out a small stack of hundreds.

"What's this for?" I asked while I counted. "There is fifteen hundred dollars here. Why would you give me all this money?" I asked with a big smile.

"Your father didn't want you to work while getting your education. I know you have a few weeks before you will be attending classes again, but I want you to quit that dirty-ass factory job now. You won't need to work until you graduate. Daddy had fifty thousand dollars put up in the safe when he passed away. I didn't need it for anything. He made sure we were taken care of financially. So, go to your job today with your resignation," she said as she cleared our dishes from the island.

I helped her wash them and tidy up the kitchen. "Thank you for everything you do for me. I love you so much!" I hugged her and kissed her on the cheek. "You know, I have saved ninety percent of my earnings. I have seventy-eight thousand dollars in my savings account," I said.

"Good for you, Rita. Mama's proud of ya, baby!" she said. "And I love you too. Have a good day."

I took care of business, resigned from my job, and spent two hours enrolling for the spring semester. It was eleven o'clock in the morning by the time I finished, and I knew I had missed Gus at the diner. I decided to go to the library and do some research, looking at newspaper articles on missing people.

No information about a missing young woman had been reported for the past forty-five years. I didn't know where to begin to find out who the blonde was.

Oh, my brain was starting to ache. I was going home to have lunch and relax my mind while I waited for Tara to come over.

I walked in our back door to find my mom talking to someone I'd not met before. "Hello, Rita," Mom said.

"Hey," I said as I walked to the kitchen.

"This is my old friend Richard from high school," Mom said. I gave the man a warm smile and opened the fridge to retrieve sandwich supplies.

"Richard retired from the FBI a few months back, and he has come back home to live. He is looking for a house to buy," Mom said. I made my ham-and-cheese sandwich and sat at the island with Mom and Richard.

Mom was acting funny. There was definitely a nervous vibe coming from her. I would find out later what was going on. I ate my sandwich in silence and observed Richard while my mom chatted about one topic or another.

"I am going up to my room to wait for Tara to come over. Nice to meet you, Richard," I said.

"You too, Rita," he replied.

I closed my bedroom door and lay across my bed to relax. Maybe I would take a short nap.

"Rita," Tara said, sitting on my bed.

"What time is it?" I asked.

"Four thirty. I had a video conference with the corporate office today," she said.

I sat up and asked, "What was it about?"

Tara looked like she had been crying, so I knew it wasn't good news. "The Seventy-Six truck stop is closing in six months. Corporate sold the land for interstate expansion," she said.

"Oh, honey, I'm sorry to hear that. Man, that place was built before they finished building I-65 through there," I said. Now I felt her pain too.

"Yeah, and I have put eight years of my life into the place," she said.

"I know, and you will find a better job. Now you have manager experience for your résumé," I said in an upbeat tone. "And, Tara, it's never too late to further your education."

She smiled a little. "Yeah, I know. I'm just not very book smart. I barely graduated from high school."

"We can go together. I'm sure the university has something you like to do," I said.

"Okay, I will think about it. I don't feel like shopping right now," she said.

"Was there a man downstairs?" I asked.

"No, I don't think so. Yo mama got a boyfriend?" she asked.

"I think she is seeing this guy who was here earlier. His name is Richard, and he is a retired FBI agent."

"Oh wow. That's juicy," Tara said, and we both laughed.

"I will be over at your house soon. I'm going to talk to my mom. I will get the info on this guy," I said.

I walked down with Tara. Mom was on the couch watching *Judge Judy* on TV. "Bye, honey," my mom said to Tara as she shut the door behind her.

"So, Mom, who is this guy, Richard?" I asked while sitting on the end of the couch.

"Well, he was a friend of your dad's back in high school. I ran into him at Walmart a few days ago."

"Oh," I said. "Yeah, Richard is nice looking for an old guy," I said, looking at Mom.

She smiled at me. "I'm going out with him Saturday night," she said, giggling. "Oh yeah, I made plans to go camp out in the forest this weekend. You'll have the house to yourself on Saturday night."

We both giggled.

"I'm going over to Tara's house for a bit," I said as I got up.

"Okay, baby," she replied.

Sandy was sitting on her porch swing, next to the old scarecrow when I walked toward her sidewalk. "Hello," she said. "Come on in. She's in her room."

"Okay. How are you today?" I asked.

"I'm fine. Thinking about painting the trees on a canvas."

"We have a spectacular color this year," I said as I strolled into the house.

"Hey, girl," I called out in her doorway.

"Hey. I'm starving. You want some pizza?" she asked.

"Sounds good. You know what I like on mine. I need to use the restroom." Tara nodded as she was waiting for them to take our order over the phone.

I looked in the mirror while washing my hands, and I could see my old self coming back to life. I was going to be all right.

I walked back to her bedroom and flopped down on her beanbag. "Tara, you remember that psychic we visited that time with Lizzy?" I asked.

"Yeah, Isabella. We video chat sometimes. Why?" she asked.

I made eye contact with Tara. "I wonder if I could see her and ask her to come to the Avalon with me. Jerry Lewis said I could rent room one this weekend if it's vacant," I said.

"Okay, let's see if she will answer a video call."

Isabella answered, and Tara asked her how she was doing, and if we could come for a visit. "You remember my friend Rita?" Tara asked as she held her phone up to get me on the screen also.

"Oh yes. It was a long time ago," Isabella said. "You can come over around seven tomorrow evening. Is that good for you?"

"Yes, we will see you then," Tara replied.

I filled Tara in on my quest to gather information about the blonde from my dreams. "Your pizza is here," Sandy hollered from the front door.

We ate in the dining room with Sandy. I told them about Mom's friend Richard. They agreed that a retired FBI agent dating my mom could be useful in exposing Avalon's secrets.

"Thank you for the pizza and calling Isabella. I can hardly wait to talk to her. I hope she will help me," I said as I gathered my phone and car keys.

Tara walked me to the door. "You're welcome. I'll text ya when I leave work tomorrow," she said.

"Okay. Good night."

Gathering Information

I decided to see Jerry Lewis again. I pulled my Mustang into the Avalon and parked next to his truck.

I walked into the office, finding him watching *The Price Is Right*. "Hello, young lady." He was drinking his lunchtime beer.

"Hey, Jerry," I said, leaning on the counter. "I stopped by to see if I can rent my old room for the weekend. I have the cash with me," I said.

"Oh yes. It will be sixty for the two nights," he said. He started filling out a receipt.

"Jerry, I'm doing some freelance writing, and I was hoping you can help me."

"Yes, I can try," he replied.

"Okay, good. You have the time now?" I asked.

"Yes, I do. What would you like to know?"

"What was that man's name that lived here all those years?" I asked.

He said, "Harold Edwards stayed forty-three years in room one."

"Okay," I said as I wrote the information down in my notebook. "Do you know where he worked?"

"He retired from the US Postal Service. We had a retirement party for him. I think he put in thirty years," he said.

"So, why did he stay here so long?" I asked.

Jerry offered me a beer, and I took it. He held his bottle up for a "cheers," and we tapped bottles and took a big drink together.

"I guess because he never found the right girl to marry. He was a Vietnam vet, just come back from his tour when he rented his room here. His attitude toward women wasn't healthy by no means."

"Oh," I said.

Jerry studied my reaction for a second. "I only knew the man seventeen years. He could have been a real ladies' man in his day," he said.

"Did you attend his service when he passed?" I asked.

"Sure did. He was a highly decorated vet, and he had a full military honors funeral," he said.

"Well, I am impressed. I wish I had met the man. He is going to be the center of the article I am working on. I need to get going. Thank you so much for your time. I will see you in two days."

"All right, young lady. You have safe travels now."

I typed "Harold Edwards" in the search bar on my laptop. There were only ten thousand Harold Edwardses to choose from. Hopefully, a little information would narrow down my search. I entered our town and state. Then I saw an obituary for Harold Edwards with a picture of him. *Wow* was all I could think.

He was born January 4, 1949, and died January 3, 2012, with no surviving relatives, and never married. He retired from the US Postal Service in 2001, with thirty years of service. In his picture, he was a nice-looking man. He kind of looked like Clint Eastwood. I didn't see where ol' Harold would've had troubles attracting women.

My mom hollered up the stairs, "Rita!"

"I will be right down," I hollered back. As I came down the stairs, I could hear Richard talking in the kitchen.

"Hello, Rita," Richard said.

"Hey, how are you doing today?" I asked.

My mom interrupted. "Richard found a house and placed a bid on it." She had excitement in her voice.

"That's awesome," I said with a smile.

Richard looked happy to find a home. Mom said he was staying in a hotel by I-65.

"What street is the house located on?" I asked.

"Over on Michigan Avenue," Richard answered as he helped Mom put groceries away.

Umm, how does he know where canned goods belong? I wondered. The little things I noted in my memory bank. Yup, I thought Richard had been around here before.

"So, Richard, you retired from the FBI. How long were you an agent?" I asked.

"I gave them thirty-two years. I loved it, but I am getting too old for the job," he answered.

"Mom says y'all went to school together," I said.

"Yes, we did, and your father was my best friend. He roped in the prettiest girl in our class. After graduation, I joined the FBI after four years in the navy," he replied with a big smile, looking at my mom.

"Someday you will have to tell me what my dad was like back in y'all's day," I said.

"Rita, before I forget, Chris has called the house a couple of times this week. I'm sorry I didn't let you know. He sounded well, and here is his new number."

"Thanks, Mama. I will get back to him. I'm waiting for Tara to get off work. Oh, Tara was told the Seventy-Six is shutting down for good in six months," I reported.

"Well, that's a shame. That place was the first truck stop built after I-65 was completed. My dad used to take us in there and get postcards for a dime, and they had postage on them too," my mom said.

"Yup, they sure did," Richard said.

"I will see you two after a while. Have a nice evening," I said. I went back to my room and printed out all the information I'd found on Harold Edwards. That was something to show Isabella tonight. I dialed Chris's number and saved it to my contacts while I waited for him to answer. "Hello," he answered.

"Hey, Chris, how ya doing?" I asked.

"I'm doing better these days. How about you?"

"I feel like moving forward now. I'm socializing again. The third anniversary of the bus crash showed me that time flies on by whether we participate or not."

"Yeah, I agree. I'm clean and sober. Four months strong now. I would like to see you and catch up," he said.

"Tomorrow afternoon is good for me. You want to come over or meet out somewhere?" I asked.

"I can pick you up, and we'll get some lunch. How about one or two in the afternoon?" he asked.

"One o'clock is good. I'll be waiting for you," I said.

"How's Tara doing?" he asked.

"She's fine. We are going out this evening, across the river. I will tell her you asked about her," I said.

"Yeah, I'd like to see her too," he said.

"Okay, are you working anywhere?" I asked.

"I have applied at Mom's Music and am waiting for a start date," he said.

"I will see ya tomorrow. Bye for now."

"Okay, Rita, I'll be there." He hung up.

Wow, it had been a year since I'd heard from him. I hoped he was moving forward too. The bus crash ended Skitch and our lives as we knew it. I had to remind myself every day that Keith and Hayden would want us all to live life to the fullest potential.

Tara came in to say hello to my mom and meet Richard when she picked me up to go see Isabella. I put on the jumpsuit Keith got me. I know it may sound silly, but I felt Keith when I wore it. Besides, I looked spectacular in it, the way it contoured my shape. My mom was right about looking good being part of feeling good.

"How was your day?" I asked when we pulled out of my driveway.

"It was good but sad too. I had to tell my employees the Seventy-Six is closing by May," she said.

"I'm all signed up for the spring semester. They have a program for business management. I know you would do well, with the experience you have," I encouraged.

"Okay, I will see about financial aid. My mom used my college money on updating the house."

"Dammit, she didn't want that money to sit and draw interest," I said, laughing.

"Well, she knew college was not on my agenda," she said.

We stopped at the Seafood Place to eat. I got some crab legs and had to use a bib to keep my outfit from the dribbles of garlic butter. Crab legs are messy but worth every bite.

We arrived at Isabella's house a bit early, but she was glad to see us. We followed her to the kitchen, where she offered us a drink. "I will have a Coke, please," I said.

We sat down at the kitchen table, and Isabella looked at me. "I am happy to see you have decided to move forward."

How did she know that? I guess Tara had talked to her about me before.

"Yes, my love was taken three years ago now. Since he's been gone, I have struggled with wanting to live. I have a secret that I need to let go of. Once I make it right, I will be able to go on," I said.

"I'm ready to expose a murder that happened decades ago," I announced. "The victim haunted me through my dreams. She wants people to know how her life ended."

"This is why you came to see me five years ago?" Isabella asked.

"Yes," I replied. "I have rented the old sleep room I stayed in back then. Can you come there Saturday?"

"I don't drive, so what time do you want to pick me up?" she asked with a smile.

"How about noon? Can you bring a flashlight?" I asked.

"Yes, I can," she said.

I awakened that morning feeling so good about my decision to lay this secret to rest. I could hardly wait for Saturday.

I got myself together and had an early breakfast at the Seventy-Six. Gus arrived there shortly after I ordered my omelet. He sat next to me at the counter. "Good morning," he said, looking well groomed and dashing in his gray pin-striped suit and shiny wing tip shoes. I had never seen him look so debonair before. He looked years younger.

"Oh my, look at you! If only you were forty years younger, I could fall madly in love," I said with a smile.

"Aww, you make an old man blush," he said.

The waitress came up to take his order.

"Gus, did you know Harold Edwards from the post office?" I asked.

"Well, yes, I did. We started around the same time. He retired in 2001, and we had a big blowout party for him. What makes you ask about Harold?" he said with intrigue in his voice.

"I'm writing an article for the *Legion* on highly decorated vets. And since he was a local hero, I thought I would do my piece on him."

"Yeah, I like that. So, what do you want to know about him?"

"What kind of man was he?" I replied.

"He was a good guy. We worked five years together until I went to the main hub for a promotion."

Our food arrived, and we both began to eat while it was hot. The omelet was the best, as usual. It was a shame this place would be torn down. It had the best breakfast in town.

"His obituary said he never married. Why do you think that is?" I asked.

"I think he was in love once with a girl named Trudy. She was from Tennessee, but I guess she didn't like him as much. He bought her a nice engagement ring, but then she ran off with another guy. Even her own cousin didn't know where she ran off to," he said.

"Oh, she had family here in town?" I asked.

"Yeah, George Wiseman and his wife, Dora. George grew up next door to me. I didn't like him much. He became a real asshole in high school. Don't know what Dora saw in him."

"He still around?" I asked.

"Naw, that bastard died ten years ago. Love is blind, some say …"

"So, do you remember what Trudy looked like?" I asked.

"She was absolutely, breathtakingly beautiful. Long blonde hair, big green eyes. The same as yours," he said.

Chills ran up my spine. *Oh shit …*

"Thank you so much for the information. I hope to write a prize-winning article about Harold Edwards," I said.

"He deserves that for his service in Vietnam. I couldn't go because I'm flat-footed," he said. Then he followed up with, "I was lucky." Yeah, I would have to agree with that.

"Why are you dressed up today?" I asked.

"Because I'm going to a retirement party for one of my postal sisters tonight. This morning I tried on my suit and decided to look debonair all day," he said as he reached for his fedora.

"Well, I love the outfit on ya," I said as I hugged him. He picked up my check and gave me that look. "Thank you, Gus."

I typed "Dora Wiseman" into the search bar. Only one popped up on the screen. Her last known address was 109 West Gilmore Avenue. Okay, that search was easy. I hoped she still lived there.

I knocked on the door and rang the doorbell, thinking this lady was slow moving. Sure enough, after the third knock, she pulled her curtain back to see me.

The door opened. "May I help you?"

"Are you Dora Wiseman?" I asked.

The lady opened the door more and said, "Yes, I am."

"I would like to ask you a few questions about Trudy Wiseman," I said.

She opened the storm door and invited me in. "You can have a seat. Would you like some hot tea?" Then her teapot whistle started blowing.

"Yes, ma'am, that would be nice," I said. I sat down and looked around the room. There were lots of plants sitting around. She had a green thumb for sure.

Dora had a tall, slender build. As she set her silver tea tray down on the coffee table, I could see she had pretty true-blue eyes. She was a very attractive woman for her age. "Would you like sugar cubes?" she asked.

"Yes. Two, please," I replied. She handed me a cup on a saucer, and then she dropped two cubes in the steamy tea. "Thank you," I said.

"Boy, I haven't thought of her in a long time. She was my husband's cousin," she said. "Why are you interested in Trudy?"

I had to think quick for an answer. "I was adopted, and in search of my birth parents, her name came up. She may be my grandmother," I said.

"Oh goodness. Well, I know she grew up in Cross Plains, Tennessee. My husband's father's side came from there. The last time we saw her was before she ran off with some guy she met up here. That was the summer of seventy-one," she said.

"So you haven't heard from her since 1971?" I asked.

"Yeah, that's right," she said.

"Okay, do you think she would have family still living in Tennessee?" I asked.

She thought for a minute and answered, "Yes, she had three brothers. Surely their kids are still around. I'm sorry, but we didn't see his people much over the years. They weren't a close family, you know?" she said.

"Yes, I know what you mean. Your tea is very good, and thank you so much for talking with me. At least I know where to begin tracing down my birth parents now," I said.

"You're welcome. Did your adopted parents give you a good life?" she asked.

"Oh yes, the best. I'm just curious about who made me and where I get my looks from. My parents are African American, so I don't favor either one of them," I said. Dora chuckled at my humor.

"Well, honey, I wish you luck on your quest," she said. She walked me to the door. "If you find out we are related, please come back and let me know. I would be honored to have such a beauty like yourself added to our family," she said with a warm smile.

"Yes, ma'am, I will."

I had time to go home and write down all the information I had so far. I remembered Chris was coming over at one o'clock. I had forty minutes before he was due to arrive.

Chris knocked on the back door right on time. He stepped in and picked me up for the biggest bear hug. "You're squeezing me," I said.

"I'm sorry, but God, it's good to see you, Rita," he said, putting me back down on my feet. He was a six-foot-two and about 250-pound teddy bear who played a mean electric guitar. That was the best description of him. He'd learned to play guitar in third grade and was self-taught. Then he helped Keith learn bass by middle school. Hayden learned drums from being in our marching band in high school. Sam met the group our senior year. He was now in New York working on whatever.

"Chris, you look great!" I said.

"You do too. Where would you like to eat lunch?" he asked.

"How about the Waffle House?" I said. We climbed up in his monster Dodge truck, he started the engine, and Saliva was cranked up loud. I loved that band!

"Yeah," he hollered as we rolled down my street. Waffle House was packed, and we had to wait a bit for a table to open. We shared a cigarette outside the door while we waited. "You know, since I got clean, the world has looked different to me. I have learned appreciation for being able to live my life. Keith and Hayden loved life and had so much to live for. They got cut short, and I lived. I guess that's why I sunk deep into using after they died," he said.

He opened the door just as soon as the first table became vacant. As we sat down, the waitress came right over to us.

"I want a sweet tea," I told the waitress. Chris wanted the same.

I picked up his hands and said, "I'm glad you came out of that fog! You have so much to live for too. I think those of us left behind after that bus crash have a duty to Keith and Hayden to live our lives to the fullest. I realized that about two weeks ago," I said.

The waitress delivered our drinks and was ready to take our orders. "I'll have a double cheeseburger with smothered hash browns," Chris said.

"I'll take a waffle with extra butter, please," I said.

"You know, right before the accident, Tara and I were talking through emails. I wanted to spend time with her, and I think she felt the same. I wonder if I still have a chance with her," he said.

"I didn't know you two were talking back then. But you won't know until you try, right?" I asked.

He thought about it and then said, "I think I will try to feel her out. You think Tara would be cool if I just dropped by her house?"

"Yeah, I think she would be okay with that idea," I replied.

Our food was delivered, and my waffle was so good. It had been a long time since I'd had one. Chris ate his burger in deep thought. I could tell the wheels in his head were turning hard.

"I'm going back to school to finish my degree in journalism. Then I'm going to travel the world reporting the news. Keith and I talked a lot about the places we wanted to visit," I said.

"Well, I don't have a plan for the rest of my life. I'm working on a day-by-day basis here," he said.

I laughed at that statement. "I know what you mean there."

"Rita, I need to be back with my real friends. Getting clean left me friendless. I can't believe I spent all my money on getting everyone high. Now, none of them are around," he said.

"Well, we'll be right here for ya. All you have to do is come around. You are welcomed back with open arms, my friend."

Chris dropped me off at home and said he would call me later on.

Tara strolled through my bedroom door.

"Hey, girl, how was your day?" I asked.

"Did you see Gus today?" she asked.

"Yes, I did. I didn't know it was him at first. I was amazed by the way he cleans up. I mean, he even got the hair out of his ears," I said, laughing.

"Where was he going today?" she asked.

"He said a retirement party for one of his postal sisters. I gather they throw retirement parties for everyone who makes it to retirement. He told me he felt like looking debonair all day," I replied.

"Well, he sure did," she said.

"Sit down a sec. I want to tell you what I have learned about the blonde." I patted the bed for her to sit. She grabbed the candy dish for some M&Ms before flopping on my bed.

"Her name is Trudy Wiseman, and I got that name from Gus. The man who lived for forty-three years in the sleep room was Harold Edwards. I got that from Jerry Lewis," I said.

Tara's eyes were wide looking at me. "Shit, is all I can say," she responded.

"Yup, me too. Blown away the couple in my dreams have names now," I said. "Was Richard here when you got here?"

"No, your mom was in the greenhouse working."

"He's been here a lot this week. They have a date for Saturday. I told Mom I was going camping in the forest. She was happy to have the house alone for the weekend," I said.

"Okay, I am I going camping with you?" she asked.

"Yes. And I hope you stay with me at the Avalon. Isabella should tell us what to do next. I think my mom having a retired FBI agent for a boyfriend is awesome. Whenever I get the facts together, I'm turning it all over to him."

"Sounds like a plan, Stan," she said.

"You wanna smoke some tree?" she asked while retrieving a big blunt from her cigarette pack.

"I have not smoked in three years," I said.

"I know. I need it right now. All day I had to answer questions from the staff about our closing. Also had a few reference inquiries about my staff. They may all jump ship before May," she said with sadness.

She fired up that blunt, and after two big hits, I was higher than a kite. Tara was too. We laughed about all our problems. At one moment we both had tears streaming down our faces.

I lit some candles for the odor and said, "Mom will be up here if she smells this stuff all upstairs." We laughed some more because Mom is funny when we're high …

"I miss the life I had before the bus crash," I said.

"I know. But now we both are on new paths. It's all good, Rita."

Tara hugged me, and I felt her strength. "I know it's good to get rid of the bad shit," I said.

"You hungry?" she asked.

We made our way to the kitchen. Mom came in the back door. "I am making chili for dinner," she said. She looked at us and started laughing. "You two got the munchies? I can have chili ready in a couple of hours. Try some fruit." She handed us the bowl with oranges and apples in it. We each grabbed an apple.

"Hey, Mom, can we have a Halloween party this year?"

"Okay, I'm up for that. It's next weekend, so maybe y'all would like to go shopping for the supplies we need?" Mom asked.

"We can do that. You make us a list, and we can go right now," I said.

We had good conversation with Mom while eating chili, and she made the best. Richard stopped by to say he closed on the house on Michigan Avenue. My mom looked so tickled over his news, and she got up and gave him a kiss and a hug. I wondered when they planned to tell me how deep their relationship really was. She needed to have a good man in her life. Seven years was a long time to be alone. I was happy for her. I was going to go get my career and travel around the world. Keith would want me to fulfill some of our dreams.

"Tomorrow is the big day," I said to Tara.

"Yup, you ready for all this?" she asked.

"Yes, I'm ready. This secret was long overdue to come out. Trudy Wiseman will be set free from the Avalon. May her soul find its peace," I said.

"Get a good night's sleep, and come over in the morning to get me," she said.

"Okay, good night," I said as I walked her to her car in the driveway.

I packed up a sleeping bag and some clothes for the weekend before going to bed. I lay there for hours, thinking about Trudy Wiseman and Harold Edwards. I knew there would be no justice for Trudy, since her killer was dead. I hoped telling the world about the cave would release her soul …

Autumn leaves were blown off the trees during the night. This October had had eighty degree temperatures until this cold front moved in. I was glad summer had ended finally. I dressed in jeans and a sweatshirt for comfort. I did a quick check on the supplies I packed for this venture. I actually found three flashlights that worked.

I went to my mom's room to let her know I was leaving. "Hey, Mom, can I come in?" I asked.

"Hold on a second," she responded. I turned the knob, and it was locked. She opened the door. "Good morning, baby. You leaving now?" she asked.

"Yeah, I have my phone but can't get a good signal in the forest. I will be back tomorrow," I said.

"Okay, y'all be careful. I love you."

"Love you too. Have fun on your date tonight," I said.

I went on my way. My mom was so funny. She never locked her bedroom door. I was pretty sure Richard was in her bathroom. It was silly to hide the fact that he spent the night. I would address this issue later. At twenty-four years old, I was old enough to realize my mom needed a man in her life. She still treated me like a kid sometimes.

I arrived at Tara's house. Sandy was fixing bacon and eggs for us. "Mom wants to go with us," Tara said.

"Okay, I'm good with that. I need to go to the Avalon to check in alone. While I do that, can y'all pick up Isabella?" I asked.

"Okay, we can meet back here. I'll text ya when we come back across the bridge," she said.

We had a good breakfast and parted ways. I arrived at the Avalon to see Jerry Lewis. "Good morning, young lady," Jerry said.

"Good morning. I know I'm a bit early for check-in, but I wanted to get out of the house before the relatives showed up," I said.

He laughed as he handed me the key to room 1. My hand was shaking as I took the key. "You feeling all right?" he asked with concern.

"Yeah, I need to eat something," I said to cover my feelings. My hands were shaking at the thought of going back down that tunnel. "It's all good, Jerry," I assured him.

I put the key in the door and turned the knob. The room was absolutely the same as it had been five years ago. I sat down on the bed and looked in the mirror. "I'm back to help you this time, Trudy," I said out loud.

My phone vibrated in my back pocket, and I jumped out of my skin. Tara texted to let me know they would be arriving at her house soon. I left the Avalon to meet them.

I gotta get a hold of my nerves right now, I told myself on the drive back to Tara's house. I wanted to free myself from the past, move on with a clear conscience. Thank goodness this was a short ride. I could have had a nervous breakdown any minute.

I got back first, so I went to the backdoor sat on the swing to wait. My hands were still shaking as I lit a cigarette.

Sandy walked around the corner of the yard. "You okay, honey?" she asked me.

"Yeah, I'm good," I lied.

We all went in the house, and Sandy made some hot tea while we discussed the possibility of the bones even still being there.

"I think it's all still there, the tunnel and cavern," Sandy said, and Tara agreed with her.

"If someone other than that Jerry character discovered bones in a cave, it would have been on local news. Don't y'all think?" Sandy asked.

"Yes, I think you're right," Isabella said.

"I'm ready. Let's do this," I said.

We loaded up in my Mustang and headed to the Avalon.

"Before we get there, I must tell you that I'm not a psychic. I don't foresee the future. I use that term to make money on the side. I see ghosts, and the dead can communicate with me," Isabella said to the group.

"Oh, well, that's even better," I said.

"Yes, that is," Sandy agreed.

"Good. I don't tell people this fact about me because of the ridicule I had to hear growing up. I was seven the first time I was haunted by a ghost. When I told my mother that we had a ghost in the house, she dismissed it. She told me not to make up such stories. So I have always kept this to myself," Isabella said.

"Don't they scare you?" I asked.

"Not like it used to when I was a child. They mean no harm to the living. Most of them are wanting to cross over and need guidance, or they have unfinished business with the living. There are also times like this one. Trudy wants her remains to be laid to rest in the proper way," she said.

"There are at least fifty souls trapped in that cave. If we help one, we help them all," Isabella announced.

"Okay, we can do that," Tara said.

Isabella said, "I feel much better letting you all know about me. I am glad I can help you and help Trudy find her way back home."

We entered room 1, and we all found a seat. I had pulled the old rug aside and exposed the cellar door. "Let's get the bags out of my truck and go down there," I said.

"Okay, let's do this," Sandy said. She followed me out to the parking lot.

Isabella, sitting on the bed, facing the mirror on the dresser, seemed to be in a trance. Tara called her name, and her eyes wouldn't leave the mirror. My heart felt like it was going to beat out of my chest. I wondered what Isabella saw in the mirror.

Isabella looked at me and said, "Trudy wants to go home."

I looked at Isabella and said, "We can do that. Let's go down here and see if the bones are still there." I opened the cellar door, and we walked down with flashlights in hand. Everything looked the same except all the spiderwebs.

Tara says, "Oh shit, this is creepy."

"I totally agree," Sandy chimed in.

We made a path through the webs to the tunnel entrance. "Rita," I heard a faint voice say.

I felt a cold breeze pass my body. I turned around and shined my light on Tara's face. "Did you feel that?" I asked.

"Yeah, I felt the cold," she said.

"Look up," Isabella said.

We all saw the ball of light hovering above us. It was Trudy lighting our way. We made our way to the cavern, and it looked the same. We walked in for a better view.

Sandy gasped and dropped her flashlight. "Oh my God, there's a skull." I picked up her flashlight and handed it to her. "Yes, like I told you, there are piles of bones," I said.

Isabella said, "Trudy, show us were your remains are." A bright flash of light passed our heads and led out of the cavern. We following the light to where it stopped, behind the cellar steps.

A wooden box, about five feet long, sat behind the steps. We pulled it out and opened it. A skeleton lay wearing a long white dress surrounded by plastic flowers. "Y'all think we could get this box up the steps?" Sandy asked.

"I have a bag we can just put her bones in," I said.

"Okay, go get it," Tara said.

I went up the steps for the duffel bag. The four of us tried to pick up her remains carefully, but we dropped some of the skeleton on the ground. We placed the bones in the bag as delicately as possible.

We came back up the steps back into the room. "I gotta pee right now!" Sandy said as she closed the bathroom door.

"I hear ya, Mom. Seeing ghosts scares the piss out of me too," Tara said. "So should we take her bones to Tennessee?" Tara asked the group.

"Yes, we should. Her soul needs to rest in peace," Isabella said.

"I'm telling Richard all about the cave tomorrow. It will take months for the FBI to identify all the victims after they find the bones. We have Trudy's, so we can do this today. Hell, it's only one o'clock now. Tennessee is only three hours away," I said.

"I'm sorry, but I can't go to Tennessee today, ladies. Call me later and I will let you know," Isabella said.

"We don't know where her home is, or if she has any family left," Sandy said.

"Well, I met her cousin who lives in town. I know Trudy's home is in Cross Plains, Tennessee. They had a big family farm," I said.

"Okay, I think we should take the road trip and find out if she has a relative left. Just go from there. What do you think, Rita?" Tara asked.

"Yeah, I'm ready to go back to your house," I replied. "Okay, let's put her remains in the truck. Let's fix the rug back over the cellar door before we leave."

"This is some crazy shit here. All those bones and a serial killer no one ever knew about. Right here in our little home town," Sandy said.

"Right …" said Tara.

The Way It Works Out

We arrived back at Sandy's house and all went inside. As we sat at the kitchen table, Sandy said, "We need to iron out this story to tell Richard." She glanced around the table. "Do you plan to tell him you have known of this cavern graveyard for five years, Rita?"

"I was going to tell the truth," I replied.

"What about the other souls trapped inside the cave?" Tara asked.

"Well, I think once the remains are taken out of the cave, their souls will be released," Isabella answered.

We sat there in silence while Sandy made some hot tea. We all needed to calm ourselves and think clearly on what the next step should be. "I don't think revealing the whole truth to Richard is a good idea," Sandy said as she sat down at the table. We all had a steamy cup of tea in front of us.

"I think you should tell him we found that cave by accident," said Sandy.

"Okay. I'm all for that, but we don't know where it leads to," I said.

"We need to go back and find our way out. There has to be an entrance somewhere. I know there is. We used to go cave exploring back in the day all around the rock quarry on the other side of town," Sandy said.

"Let's do it! Mom, what equipment do we need?" Tara asked.

Sandy made a list for this adventure. Then Isabella said, "I wish I could go with ya, but I need to be home soon."

Sandy spoke up and said, "There are about three hours before dark. Why don't you girls go take inventory of the equipment you already have?" Then she turned to Isabella and said, "I can take ya home, honey."

Thirty minutes later, we had most of the items on the list—plus junk food in case we got hungry. We needed to stop for extra batteries on our way to the Avalon, though. "I'm going to give you three hours to call me. If you don't, I will come to that room. Leave that door unlocked," Sandy said.

Tara gave her mom a big hug. "It's all good. I love you, Mom," Tara said.

I hugged them both, and Isabella followed for a group hug. "Thank y'all for helping me and being there for me," I said with a tear in my eye.

I handed her the watch to set the timer. She handed it back and said, "You want me to roll some tree? Make it a real adventure."

I couldn't help but giggle. "Okay, hurry up. I will send your mom a text letting her know we are going in five minutes," I said.

I pulled the rug back and opened the cellar door. Tara finished and handed me a big fatty. "You know two hits off this and I'll be higher than Coody Brown," I said.

She started giggling. "Come on, I'm ready," she said.

We stopped to look at our reflections in the dresser mirror. "We look ready for a covert ops mission, don't we?" she said.

"Yup, let's go." I made sure we left the room unlocked for Sandy.

"Ready," we both said, heading down the steps.

We had headband flashlights along with big Maglights in hand illuminating the room. We slowly scanned the cavern from ceiling to floor. We saw stalactites hanging, along with some bats over in a corner. The bones lay around the firepit circle. Isabella said there were at least fifty victims who had entered room 1 and never came out. "Oh I got the heebie-jeebies bad right now."

"Me too," I said.

Looking around, I could see at least two paths out. "Let's try this one first," she said as she walked in that direction. I followed.

"You know who wants to see you again?" I asked her.

"No. Who?" she asked.

"Chris," I answered.

"Really?" She stopped and turned around with a surprised look on her face.

"Yeah. So let's find our way out so you guys can reconnect," I said. "Okay," she said.

I glanced at the time. So far it had been forty-nine minutes. I hoped we would find an entrance soon. "Let's stop a minute. I want to fire up that joint," Tara said.

My legs were starting to feel tired, so I sat down on a stalagmite. Tara joined me. She lit up her tree, and after taking a big drag, she passed it to me. I took a big toke and then coughed my head off. I handed it back, saying, "I don't need any more of that."

"I'm ready to go now," Tara said, standing up to lead the way.

"Man, I got a buzz off that one hit," I said.

"Yeah, me too," she responded.

We walked around a corner on the path, and we heard a muffled noise. It sounded like a train. We both thought we knew where we were. A train track ran along the interstate for a couple of miles. We started walking faster, and we finally reached an entrance. We came out under a train trestle that ran parallel to I-65. I pulled my phone out to call Sandy.

I walked up the hill to the train track. I could see the back of the Avalon in the distance, and I-65 was about a mile away in the opposite direction. I could also see a small access road a few hundred feet away. Sandy answered her phone, telling me she was already back at the Avalon. I described my location to her, and she knew exactly where we were. She told me to walk to the access road and she would be there very soon.

We reached the road pretty quickly, and then we sat down on a log to wait for Sandy. "My legs are so tired," I complained.

"Mine are too. I'm glad Mom is coming. It would suck to have to walk back to the Avalon," she said.

Sandy picked us up. As we drove down the access road, she told me how she got there. "When you go north on Highway 31 through town, turn left on Peach Street. Then you follow it all the way to the end, where the access road begins. You guys were about a quarter mile down the access road."

"Let's spend the night in that room, for old time's sake. Please?" Tara asked as we pulled up at the Avalon.

"OMG, let me think on that for a second," I replied. "I'm hoping Richard will be at my house in the morning. This is some crazy shit I'm about to tell him. For tonight, I'm chilling with my bestie, and I want some wine …"

Tara was disappointed when I strongly objected to sleeping at the Avalon tonight. I told her, "It's bad enough that I have a skeleton in a duffel bag riding along in the truck. I'm not up for crazy dreams. I need some rest."

We had some wine, and Sandy tried to talk me into using a Ouija board for fun. "No, no fucking way!" I said. Tara was freaked out by the idea also.

"Let's video chat with Isabella," I suggested.

"Okay," Tara said. She went searching for her tablet, while I poured another glass.

"Tell me what you're going to tell Richard in the morning," Sandy said.

"I'm going to tell him we were exploring a cave yesterday and stumbled upon this graveyard in the middle cavern," I said.

Then Sandy said, "I'm happy for you. I'm excited to see what you do next. Life is magical, and every morning is a fresh start."

"We have Isabella on the screen," Tara announced. We sat on the couch and chatted with her, giving her the details of how our adventure went. Isabella said that we would go to Tennessee Tuesday morning. I was good with that plan.

I woke up on Tara's big bean bag on her bedroom floor. My head was banging from all that wine. As I was going to the bathroom, I heard Sandy making coffee in the kitchen. "Good morning, Rita," Sandy said with enthusiasm.

"Good morning. I need something for my headache, please," I said.

"You drank the two bottles we bought last night. You're funny when you're drunk. My cheeks are aching from laughing so hard," she said.

"Yeah, I remember most of our conversations. I cracked myself up last night," I said.

I looked at the time. It was only six thirty. "I am going home after one cup of coffee to see what Richard and my mom are up to. I want to catch him early," I said.

"Right," Tara said, coming into the kitchen.

"Good morning, baby. Did you sleep well?" Sandy asked her.

"Yeah, except for girlfriend's snoring. OMG, you were sawing the logs," Tara said with laughter.

"I'm sorry, bestie. I had a good buzz on," I said. I got up to move around and get my stuff together. I took some Advil for my head and drank my coffee. I listened to their chat about the plans for the day.

"I'm going with you to talk with Richard, and I'm going out to the cave with you guys," Tara said.

"Yeah, I know. I'm ready to go home. You shower up and come on over. I'll see ya later on, Sandy," I said.

An hour later my head felt much better and I was all cleaned up. I felt like a new woman. I knocked on Mom's door, and she opened the door immediately. It made me jump, and we both busted out with laughter.

"Good morning, baby," Mom said.

"Good morning. Is Richard here?" I asked.

My mother was silly at times. At first, she tried to act like he wasn't in her bathroom. I gave her a smile. "Really, Mom? I'm all grown up now. I need to speak with him when he's ready to come downstairs. I love ya, Mom," I said, walking to the staircase leading to the kitchen.

Tara arrived with perfect timing. "Did you have breakfast?" I asked her.

"No, just coffee," she replied.

"How about our favorite breakfast?" I said.

"Oh yeah, sounds good," she answered, following me to the kitchen. Fresh coffee and bakery doughnuts were a stoner's breakfast of champions.

Soon Richard came down, freshly showered, with a nice-smelling aftershave on. "Good morning, young lady," he greeted me. Sheena, our dog, was right behind him. She liked him. That was a good sign.

"What's going on, ladies? Your mom is dying to know what you need to talk to me about," he said.

I giggled. He was funny. "We went cave exploring yesterday afternoon and stumbled upon a cavern with a pile of human bones in it," I said. Tara looked at me, then shifted to Richard's reaction.

"Are you sure they are human bones?" he asked.

"We think so. We didn't touch any of them. We had good lighting with us. We know what we saw," I said.

"Well, do you know how to find it again?" he asked.

"Yes," Tara said.

"The entrance is located under a train trestle that is a few hundred feet from the access road that starts at the end of Peach Street. You're the first person I thought of last night to share this with," I said.

He stood up straight, like he thought that was cool. "Okay, let's have breakfast and get some gear together. I'll check it out before I call my buddies in the bureau," he said.

"We will be up in my room when you're ready," I said.

Mom came downstairs as we headed up to my room. As I closed my bedroom door, I heard my mom asking Richard, "What's up?"

We listened to the Switchfoot album *The Beautiful Letdown* while we waited for Richard. The song "Meant to Live" was Keith's favorite on the album. I loved it, and I could almost feel him when I listened to this album. Finally Mom knocked on my door.

"Come in," I said.

"Richard filled me in. Oh my, what a trip. My only question is, How did you go from camping to caving?" Mom said.

"Well, when we arrived at the forest, we decided it was too cold for camping," I said.

That's when Tara chimed in and said, "I suggested that we pick up my mom and go caving. She knows where all the caves are around here." Then Tara said, "What we found is some crazy shit for our little town." My mom nodded in total agreement.

Richard yelled up the stairs that he was ready to go. We headed down the stairs, and he was waiting in the living room. "Rita, you wanna drive us where we're going?" he asked.

"Yes, we are ready to go," I said.

We all hugged Mom on our way out the door.

We parked my Mustang on the side of the access road. We grabbed our backpacks and started the walk to the trestle. "So, your mom said you girls were camping in the forest last night."

"We changed our minds. It's too cold at night now," I said.

"Yeah, we haven't explored caves in a long time. My mother went with us too. She loves to hike and get out in nature," Tara said.

"Richard, I want you to know I'm happy that my mom is seeing you. So far you have my vote. I like the fact that you knew my dad. I think he would approve of you," I said.

"Thank you. We are not rushing into anything. We will take it easy and see how things develop," he assured me.

We reached the entrance, finally. "It will take about forty minutes to walk to the cavern," I said as we entered.

"Okay, I need the exercise after the meal your mom cooked last night. She is an amazing cook," he said, smiling.

"Yes, I almost forgot she loves to cook. Since Dad's passing, she has stopped creating in the kitchen. That warms my heart that she has found someone to cook for," I said.

We walked through the cave in silence for a while. We took in the beauty of the stalactites, and I pulled my phone out and took a few pictures. "Richard, how long have you and my mom been dating?" I asked him out of the blue. I could tell by his facial expression that I had caught him off guard with that question. "Truth is, we were dating while you were in school upstate. When your boyfriend passed, she told me we had to put things on hold. She wanted to be there for you," he said.

"Aww," Tara said, patting me on the back. "Both our moms are so wonderful. We are very lucky," she said.

"I would've welcomed you into our lives back then," I said.

"I'm happy to hear that. Makes me feel good. I understood what she needed from me, and it was worth the wait. She is a beautiful woman inside and out," he said with a twinkle in his eye. I liked this man.

"We are almost there," Tara said.

"Good, my legs are achy again. Let's sit here for a minute or two," I said. I ate a snack and offered Richard a water from my backpack.

"Thank you," he said.

"Let's go," Tara said.

So we finished our waters and put our trash in my backpack. Tara went ahead of us, and then I heard her voice echo, "Oh shit."

"You okay?" Richard hollered.

"Yeah, my batteries died in my flashlight," she replied.

"The extras are in your backpack," I called out.

"Okay," she said.

We caught up with her and gave her light to replace her batteries. When we reached the cavern, Richard went into FBI mode. "Don't touch nothing," he said as he shined his light around the room. "Oh my God!" he exclaimed. "I never seen anything like this before in all my thirty-two years with the bureau."

Richard didn't have much to say on the ride back home. We were gone for over three hours. Mom was anxiously awaiting our return. Richard gave her the 411 on the situation. Then he excused himself to make a phone call.

"Do you think this will make national news?" Tara asked.

"Yes, I think we will have multiple news crews in town in a few days," Mom answered.

Richard joined us at the kitchen island. "They will have a team here in the morning. I will lead them down in the cave," he said.

"Can we stay anonymous in this whole thing?" I asked him.

"I don't know about that. We will see," he said.

"Well, I'm going home. Come over soon, Rita," Tara said.

"Okay, I'll see ya," I said, walking her to the door.

"Mom, I know what's up with Richard and you. I'm totally fine with it. I like him and look forward to getting to know him. So relax, I'm happy for you two."

She looked at me with a big smile. "Okay, baby. You hungry? I will make a nice lunch for us," she said.

"I'm going to unpack my bags and stuff," I said as I walked up the stairs to my room.

A couple hours later, I walked to Tara's house to hang out for the afternoon. Tara had a joint rolled and talked Sandy into smoking with us. We laughed so hard about various topics. Watching my friends having a good time reminded me of the way my dad was. He always saw the humor in most situations. I could still hear his laugh in my head. I could only imagine what he would have to say about a bone pile deep in a cave …

"Rita," Sandy said. "I'm here."

"I was thinking about my dad," I said.

"Happy memories, I hope," Sandy said.

"Oh yeah. My dad was one of the happiest people I knew," I replied. "I'm wore out. Tomorrow is gonna be a long day. We will have to give statements and be interviewed for hours. Richard will try to keep us out of this, but I see it coming."

"Yeah, me too," Tara said.

Then I said, "I can't thank y'all enough for seeing this through with me. I love y'all."

"Aww," they said simultaneously. We did another group hug before I left to walk back home.

"See ya in the morning."

I lay on my bed, listening to music. A feeling of gratitude came over me. I was free of my regrets over the secret I carried for five years. Once I took Trudy back home to Tennessee, this would be behind me. I would have a free mind and heart to start a new path. I was so grateful for my mom and the friends I had. I fell into a peaceful slumber.

On Monday morning, I realized I hadn't checked out or left the room key at the Avalon. So I rode out there early to make sure I had all our stuff out of the room. I walked down to give Jerry Lewis the key. He answered his door in his boxers, looking hungover.

"Hey, Rita, how are you this morning?" he asked.

"I'm good. I'm sorry I took the key home with me," I said.

"No problem. Thank you for returning it to me. I'm sick. I think I got the flu," he said.

"Aww, I feel for ya." I gave him a sad face to sympathize with him.

"Come on in," he said.

"I can't right now. Got a list of things to do this morning," I said.

"Okay, young lady. Come back when you have more time to visit."

"I will soon," I promised. "Feel better soon, Jerry Lewis," I said as I walked back to the Mustang.

The sun was very bright, with a strong breeze. A hurricane was in the gulf and coming our way in a day or so. October leaves were so beautiful. There was lots of orange and yellow this year. *God, I feel so alive today.* I drove past Tara's house and her car was in the driveway, so I stopped by.

Sandy was painting in her sunroom, a beautiful scenery of autumn leaves. "Hello, Rita. How are ya?" she asked.

"I feel so good today, and you?"

"Splendid. What do you think of my work?" she asked.

"Amazingly realistic. I love it," I replied.

"Then, it shall be yours," she said, putting her brush down. "You want some tea?"

"Yes, I would love some," I replied.

"Hey, girl" Tara said from the front room.

I walked in there and sat next to her. "Why didn't you go to work?" I asked.

"'Cause I know FBI is gonna want a statement from us, so I took the day off work. The Seventy-Six crew knows to call me if they need to," she said.

"Richard went home last night. I haven't heard from him. I hope if they want to talk to us, it will be today because tomorrow Isabella and I are on a road trip. You gonna work tomorrow?" I asked.

"Yeah, I don't want to get behind for the week. You check on Trudy lately?" she asked. We both broke out in laughter.

"Yeah, I think she's still there. You so funny," I said.

I suggested we go shopping for costumes and candy to pass out on Halloween. "Okay. I'll be ready in twenty minutes," she said, getting to her feet.

I went back to the kitchen, and the teapot whistle sounded. I sat down at the kitchen table for a cup. "Thank you for the painting. I will hang it in my room," I said to Sandy. Then I told her that we were going shopping. "I may redecorate my room," I said.

"That's a good idea. Change is always good," she said.

We waited all day for Richard to call, but he didn't. We had a great shopping spree. We went to several stores. I found some orange curtains and a yellow-and-orange comforter set to match Sandy's artwork on my wall. It looked like a new bedroom. My mom knocked on my door.

"Come in," I said.

"Richard will be here shortly to fill us in on what's going on. I think I want Swedish meatballs for dinner."

"That sounds good," I said.

"I love the new colors in here. Where did you get that painting?" she asked.

"Sandy's artwork," I replied.

"She is an amazing artist. She needs to put her artwork out there," Mom said. I agreed with her.

Richard arrived for dinner with an expensive bottle of wine for us to try. He and I waited for dinner on the couch with Sheena laying on us. "I reported to the bureau that I stumbled upon the crime scene while cave exploring with my girlfriend. Of course, we will never discuss this matter with anyone," he said, making eye contact with me.

"Yes, I understand. Thank you very much," I said

We enjoyed our meal with good conversation. Richard was a good fit for my mom. She had that twinkle in her eyes again. Maybe whoever says we get only one true love in a lifetime is wrong.

Closure for Trudy

"Rita, wake up. Come downstairs and watch the local news with me." Mom was all excited, and it was still dark outside.

"Okay, what time is it?" I asked.

"Five twenty-two a.m. Come on." She had coffee ready for me, so I could peel my eyelids open. "Oh, here it is. All three networks of news crews are flying around in helicopters. Ten different law enforcement agencies are surrounding the cave entrance under the train trestle," Mom said.

"Wow. I need to text Tara to see if she has seen this yet. My new friend Isabella and I are going to drive to Tennessee today. We should be back before dark."

"What you going down there for?" she asked.

"Isabella asked me drive her down there to see her grandmother. She doesn't have a driver's license," I said.

"Please drive safe. If you spend the night, let me know. I love you, baby," Mom said, kissing my forehead. "You want some bacon and eggs to start your day?" she asked.

"Yeah, that sounds good," I replied.

After I picked up Isabella, I entered "Cross Plains, Tennessee" on the GPS. The travel time was three hours. That gave us plenty of time to figure out what we were going to say to Trudy's family.

Isabella turned to me and said, "Trudy came to me in a dream Sunday night. She showed me a willow tree by a brown barn, which is where she would like her resting place to be. This location is in the middle of the farm. The dream was very vivid."

"Yes, I still remember all those dreams I had that summer sleeping at the Avalon," I said. "I'm pretty sure the reason that Trudy reached out to me was because I was the first person to live in room one after Harold Edwards passed away. I'm also pretty sure he's the one who dug that tunnel out of that cellar.

"Earlier today, I googled the population of Cross Plains, and it said seventeen hundred thirty-one people in the town. Robertson County is seventy thousand one hundred eighty according to the 2016 census report," I said.

"Very interesting. My guess is everyone in this town knows everyone else. We should find the farm fairly easy," she said.

Cross Plains was the first exit off I-65, right over the Tennessee state line. I made good time, arriving thirty minutes ahead of schedule. We rolled into the town square and noticed a mom-and-pop kind of diner. We stopped to get some lunch. As we walked through the door, everyone was looking at us. Isabella is a child of Indian immigrants, and they were staring like they had never seen a beautiful woman of color before. The waitress was friendly and helpful and gave us directions to the Wiseman farm. I had the meatballs and spaghetti, and Isabella had tuna on rye. We agreed that the food was delicious.

The farm was on SR 25, about seven miles out of town. We pulled up to an ancient farmhouse, and we got out of the Mustang. It looked like no one was home, but we knocked on the door anyway. After the second knock, an old man came to the door.

"Hello, Mr. Wiseman," I said.

"Hello," the man said, looking confused. "Who are you?"

"I'm Rita Mason. May we come in, sir?"

He opened the door to let us in. We followed him into the front room, and he sat down in a La-Z-Boy recliner. *The Price Is Right* was playing on the TV. It appeared that he was home alone.

"My mom will be back soon. She just went to town to get supplies," he said.

This man was at least seventy years old. Isabella and I looked at each other. I looked over at him, and his pants were wet. I thought he had just urinated on himself.

"What's your name, sir?" I asked in a soothing tone.

"Curtis, Curtis Wiseman," he answered.

"Do you have a relative by the name of Trudy?" I asked.

"That's my big sister. She's at school right now," he said.

Oh shit. This man had some dementia going on. I asked him where the brown barn was. "Back behind the stables," he said.

"I hope this man doesn't live here all alone. Let's drive to the brown barn," I said to Isabella. "Curtis, is there a shovel in the barn?"

He looked confused again. "My daddy has lots of stuff in the barn."

We drove down the gravel road, and sure enough, there was a huge willow tree right by the barn. We walked into the barn. Curtis was right—the barn was piled high with everything. There was an old Texaco gas station sign, tools, and several tractors. *American Pickers* would have loved the place. Isabella found us two shovels and handed me one.

"Let's hurry up and do this," she said.

In two hours, we had successfully buried Trudy's remains. Isabella said a few words, and we bowed our heads together for a moment of silence.

"Rest in peace, Trudy Wiseman," I said.

We stopped at the farmhouse on our way out. I couldn't leave without making sure that Curtis Wiseman had changed his pants. I knocked on the door, and he came to the door with no pants on. I had to laugh. At least he'd taken his soiled pants off.

"Curtis, go put some pants on before your mom comes home," I said.

"Okay," he said and shut the door.

I jumped in the Mustang. Isabella was laughing her ass off.

"Yeah, that's some funny shit there. God love that old man," Isabella said as we headed for home.

We arrived at Isabella's house at sunset. "Thank you for all your help. We are having a Halloween party. I would love for you to come," I said.

"I would love to. Text me when you're coming to pick me up," she said as she got out of the car. The traffic was crazy in town. I was so glad to get home.

As I walked in the front door, Mom and Richard were on the couch watching the news. The boneyard cavern was now a national news story. Then I heard the reporter say, "Next up, exclusive interview with the people who stumbled upon the boneyard cavern—Richard Donovan and Kathy Mason.

I turn to my mom and said, "You guys talked to the media!"

They both looked at me with shit-eating grins. I sat down to watch the interview with them.

As it finished, Richard said, "I wonder how long it will be before someone writes a novel about this case."

I chuckled and said, "Maybe I will one day."

Printed in the United States
By Bookmasters